ALSO BY JOHN PRATER

Along Came Tom
Timid Tim and the Cuggy Thief

For Julie, Jemma and Lauren

7 9 10 8 6

Copyright © John Prater 1982

John Prater has asserted his right under the Copyright, Designs
and Patents Act, 1988 to be identified as the author and
illustrator of this work

First published in the United Kingdom 1982
by The Bodley Head Children's Books
Random House, 20 Vauxhall Bridge Road
London, SW1V 2SA

Reprinted 1983, 1987, 1991, 1993, 1998

Random House UK Limited Reg. No. 954009

A CIP catalogue record for this book is available from the
British Library

ISBN 0 370 30449 7

Printed in China

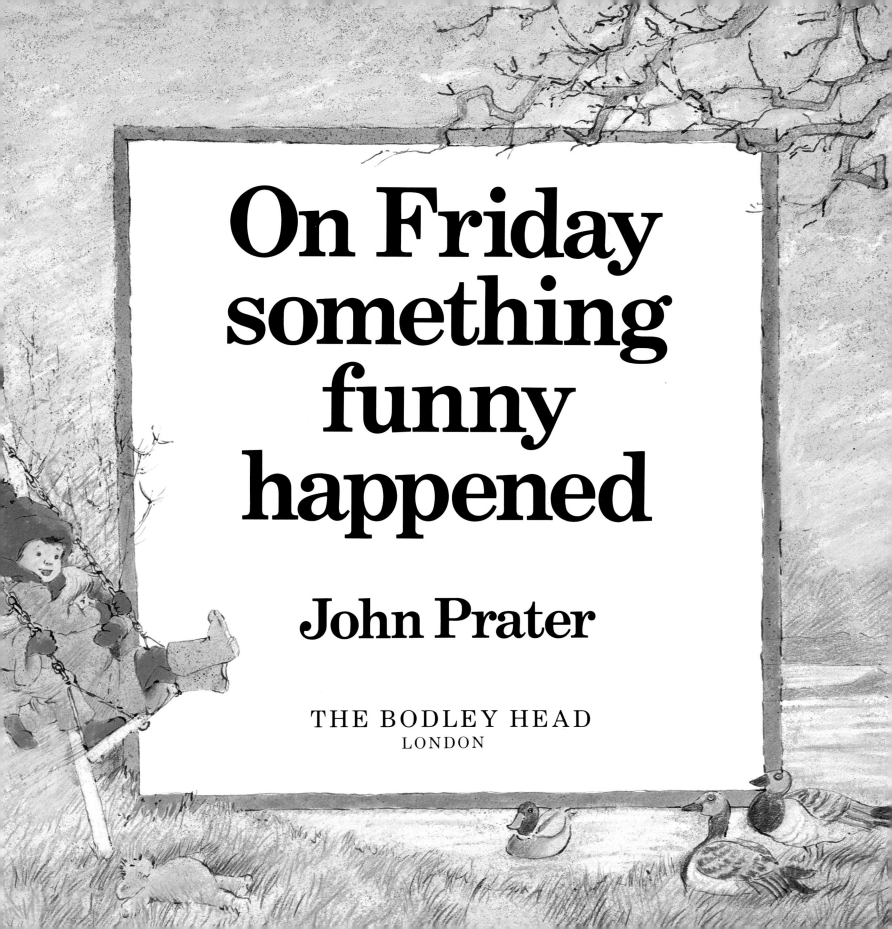

On Friday something funny happened

John Prater

THE BODLEY HEAD
LONDON

On Saturday
we went shopping.

On Sunday
we went to the park.

On Monday
we did the washing.

On Tuesday Uncle John came to lunch.

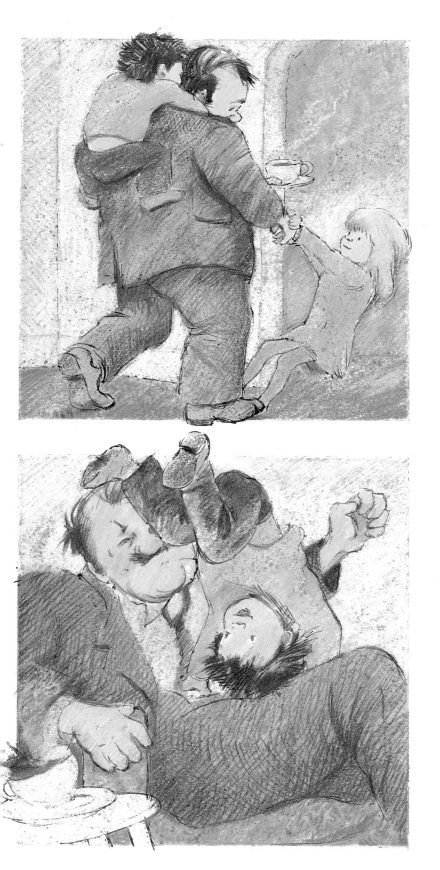

On Wednesday
we did some painting.

On Thursday we played with our friends.

On Friday something funny happened— the house was very quiet.

On Saturday we went shopping . . .